"PEE-YEW!"

Bruno Pinch wrinkled up his nose. "Miss Mombie's got really bad B.O."

"Bruno!" exclaimed Mrs. Pinch. "How very rude!"

"Sor-ry," said Bruno. "But she stinks."

Mrs. Pinch didn't want to admit it, but Bruno was right. Still, manners were manners.

"I'm so sorry," she said to Miss Mombie. "You know how boys are."

Miss Mombie glared at Bruno.

She knew just whom she was going to turn into a zombie *first*.

Critters of the Night...
they're here!

MERCER MAYER'S
CRITTERS OF THE NIGHT ™

ZOMBIES DON'T DO
WINDOWS

Written by
Erica Farber and J. R. Sansevere

Bullseye Books
Random House 🏠 New York

A BULLSEYE BOOK PUBLISHED BY RANDOM HOUSE, INC.

Library of Congress Cataloging-in-Publication Data
Mayer, Mercer.
Zombies don't do windows / written by Erica Farber and J. R. Sansevere.
    p.   cm. — (Critters of the night)
"Bullseye books."
SUMMARY: Dr. Del Ray disguises his prodigy, Zombie Mombie, as a cleaning
lady in order to gain access to the Howl residence in Critter Falls.
ISBN 0-679-87361-9
[1. Monsters—Fiction.] I. Farber, Erica II. Sansevere, J. R. III. Title IV. Series.
PZ7.F22275Zo   1996
[Fic]—dc20
95-6799
RL: 2.5
Printed in the United States of America   10 9 8 7 6 5 4 3 2 1

 A BIG TUNA TRADING COMPANY, LLC/J. R. SANSEVERE BOOK

CONTENTS

Wanda   **Jack**   **Thistle**   **Axel**

Bones

Snake

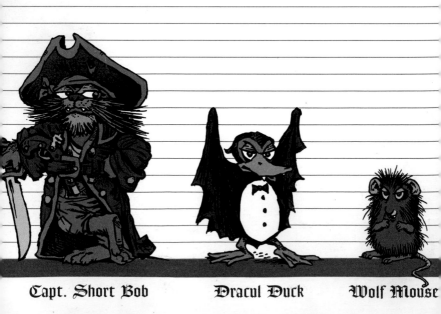

Capt. Short Bob   **Dracul Duck**   **Wolf Mouse**

Groad   Frankengator   Moose Mummy

Uncle Mole   Zombie Mombie   Auntie Bell

1

Black Magic

Many, many years ago...

By the light of the moon, a lone figure moved slowly through the jungle on a far-off volcanic island. Deeper and deeper into the jungle he went. All around him were green leaves, green bushes, green trees.

There was no road. There was not even a path. The underbrush was so thick he had to chop his way through vines and branches.

The night was silent except for the sound of his knife, slicing through the underbrush. *Swish. Swish.*

Suddenly, he stopped.

A huge stone pyramid rose up out of the jungle. The man stared up at the pyramid. Slowly, his lips curled into an evil smile.

He had finally found it—the Lost Pyramid! It was thousands of years old. Inside it lay an object many explorers had died trying to find.

It was a golden amulet of mysterious powers. It was known as the Evil Eye.

The man ran toward the pyramid. He found the door and entered.

Suddenly, drumbeats echoed through the jungle. *Boom-badda-boom-badda-boom.*

The drumbeats grew louder and louder. *BOOM-BADDA-BOOM-BADDA-BOOM!!!*

The pyramid began to shudder. It began to shake. Large gray stones came loose and crashed to the earth.

The man ran out of the pyramid. He held the golden amulet high over his head. The amulet shone in the moonlight.

At that moment, another man burst out of the bushes. "Stop right there, Del Ray!" shouted the second man.

"Nothing can stop me now, Howl!" the holder of the amulet snarled.

The island began to tremble. An army of native critters came out of the underbrush. They surrounded Del Ray and Howl. The native critters moved closer and closer. They raised their spears high in the air.

Just then, Del Ray held up the Evil Eye amulet toward the native critters.

"Don't do it!" screamed Howl, terrified. He reached out to grab the amulet.

But he was too late!

"Ana…mana…manana…" chanted Del Ray.

Suddenly, the Evil Eye opened. A strange, sickly green light shone forth.

Howl covered his eyes and prayed.

The native critters stared at the strange, sickly green light. The light washed over their bodies. Instantly, they were turned into skeletons with bloody eye sockets.

A cloud of sickly green smoke filled the air. The skeletons began to scream as the smoke swallowed them whole.

When the smoke cleared, not a single native critter was left.

All that remained were piles of dust. And a bunch of spears.

Del Ray threw back his head and laughed in triumph. His eyes glowed green. Sickly green. Just like the amulet.

"And so, Howl, the Evil Eye is now mine. All mine!" he cried. "And no one on earth can stop me..."

Howl grabbed for the Evil Eye. They struggled! The Evil Eye flew up in the air.

Just then, the island's long-dead volcano erupted. Red-hot lava poured down the mountain and streamed through the jungle.

The sound of screaming filled the air as the entire island was consumed by red-hot flames...

2

The Evil Eye

Many, many years later…

On the outskirts of the town called Critter Falls, the Howl family was enjoying a quiet evening at Old Howl Hall. They were all in the drawing room.

"My serve!" yelled young Thistle. She tossed Bones, her pet skull, up in the air. Then she swatted him hard.

"Aaahhhh!" screamed Bones as he went flying over the net.

Thistle's older brother, Axel, dived under Bones and bumped him with his head.

"Aaaahhh!" squealed Bones as he flew back over the net.

"Bones really seems to enjoy playing volleyball with the children," Jack Howl said to his wife, Wanda.

"Skulls do make wonderful pets," Wanda said. "Now, what do you think we should serve for dinner this week? Since Cousin Moose is visiting, I thought we might have something special."

"Special...," mused Jack. "How about grasshopper gumbo and jellyfish pudding for dessert? Moose does have a sweet tooth for jellyfish."

"Grrr...," grumbled Groad, the Howls' cook and butler. "Do you know how 'ard it ees to get fresh jellyfish zees time of year?"

"Now, Groad," Wanda said. "You *will* have help. The new cleaning lady will arrive in just a few days."

"Chin up, Groad," said Jack. He draped a long black cape over his shoulders. "Allow me to demonstrate one of my magic tricks."

"Grrr…," grumbled Groad. "I hate mageek."

"Where did you get that stunning cape?" Wanda asked.

"It belonged to Great-Grandpapa Howl's good friend, the late great Critterdini," explained Jack. "Great-Grandpapa met him in India years ago during one of his many trips around the world."

"Great-Grandpapa certainly was quite the explorer," said Wanda.

"That he was," agreed Jack. "And now, for my first magic trick, I will pull a rattlesnake out of this hat."

Groad and Wanda watched.

Jack pickcd up a black hat and stuck his hand inside it. Slowly, he pulled out something pink and fluffy.

"That's not a snake, dear," said Wanda,

laughing. "It's a rabbit."

"Ah, so it is!" said Jack with a chuckle. "Rabbits just don't have the charm of snakes, I'm afraid. I'll keep practicing."

"Oops!" Thistle suddenly yelled.

Just then, there was a loud crash. Bones went flying into a statue of a pink flamingo. The statue fell to the floor and shattered into tiny pieces.

"Bad shot," said Axel.

"Don't worry, children," said Wanda. "I never liked that flamingo, anyway. It was so bright and cheery-looking." She shuddered.

"True," Jack agreed. "I wonder why Great-Grandpapa had it in the first place? Pink was definitely not his color."

"Hey, look at this!" called Thistle. She pointed to a golden amulet lying on the floor in the middle of the mess. "It must have been hidden inside the statue."

"It looks like an eye," said Axel. He bent down to examine the amulet.

"Don't touch it!" Jack shouted.

"There's writing on it," Thistle went on. "It says 'Ana—'"

"Don't say it!" shouted Jack. "That's the Evil Eye—and whatever is written on it is the spell that activates its evil power."

At that moment, the Evil Eye opened. Then it mysteriously closed once again.

"What does it do?" asked Thistle.

"The Evil Eye has the power to destroy everything in the entire world," said Jack. "Including every single one of us..."

3

The Witching Hour

Meanwhile, many miles away, Dr. Del Ray pushed open the iron gate of Crittervania Cemetery.

The gate squeaked open, then slammed shut behind him.

Dr. Del Ray walked quickly along the gravel path.

Mist surrounded him as he headed farther and farther into the cemetery. A bat swooped low over his head, then disappeared into the fog.

It was midnight. The witching hour.

There was no time to lose.

He stopped in front of a small tombstone. On the tombstone was carved: ZOMBIE MOMBIE.

Dr. Del Ray looked around to make sure he was alone. Then he pulled out a small silver bell. He rang the bell three times. *Ding. Ding. Ding.* Then he waited.

A few seconds later, the earth beneath his feet began to move.

Suddenly, two arms reached out of the dirt. And something sat up. The thing smelled like death. Its arms were covered with scabs. And its eyes glowed red in the moonlight.

The thing stood up. It held out its arms, reaching toward Dr. Del Ray.

"Good evening, Zombie Mombie," said Dr. Del Ray.

Zombie Mombie didn't say anything. She just stared straight ahead, with glassy eyes.

"The time has come," said Dr. Del Ray. "Now listen carefully. You must follow my instructions exactly."

"Yes, Master," said Zombie Mombie in a hoarse voice.

"You will go to the town of Critter Falls," said Dr. Del Ray. "Critter Falls was the home of my sworn enemy, that low-down, no-good do-gooder werewolf, H. R. Howl. He's dead now. But his grandchildren live there. You will pose as a cleaning lady. They will be expecting you. They will pick you up at the bus stop."

Dr. Del Ray paused. His lips curled in an evil smile.

"You will go to their house. You will turn these Howls into zombies, one by one," said Dr. Del Ray. "Here is a bag with all the ingredients you will need." He handed Zombie Mombie a big shopping bag.

"Then you will search the house from top to bottom… until you find the Evil Eye," said Dr. Del Ray. "Howl stole it from me many, many years ago. Now I want it back!"

"Yes, Master," said Zombie Mombie.

"You will not leave without the Evil Eye," said Dr. Del Ray. "I know it is there. I can feel its power...calling out to me."

"Yes, Master," said Zombie Mombie.

"Then," Dr. Del Ray went on, "with the Evil Eye in my possession, I can turn all my enemies into worthless piles of dust. Now, go! Go to Critter Falls in your cleaning lady disguise."

Dr. Del Ray threw back his head. He stared up at the stars and laughed his evil laugh.

"Soon, I will be the master of the universe!"

4

Holy Smokes!

A few days later, Mrs. Pinch, Mrs. Pucker, and Mrs. Plum were sitting at their favorite table at the Critter Falls Cafe. It was right next to the window so they could see everything that was going on in town.

"Do you believe what those Howls did in their front yard?" Mrs. Pinch said. She took a sip of her coffee.

"Yes, I do," said Mrs. Pucker, puckering her lips. "Those Howls are creepy."

"What in the world did the Howls do now?" asked Mrs. Plum.

"They planted dead trees in their front yard," announced Mrs. Pinch.

"And their grass has grown completely wild," added Mrs. Pucker.

"Hmm...," said Mrs. Plum. "I'll have to take a look. Maybe I should let my grass grow wild."

"Beatrice Plum, you can't be serious!" scolded Mrs. Pinch.

"It's downright strange not to mow your lawn," added Mrs. Pucker. "Unheard of."

"We must do something about those Howls," said Mrs. Pinch. "They mean only one thing for this town—trouble."

"Hear, hear," agreed Mrs. Pucker.

"Oh, my!" Mrs. Pinch gasped, looking down at her watch. "I've got to run."

"But you haven't even finished your coffee," pointed out Mrs. Pucker.

"I have to pick

Bruno up at school and then go to the bus stop," Mrs. Pinch announced. "My new cleaning lady is arriving in exactly twenty minutes."

Mrs. Pucker and Mrs. Plum exchanged looks.

"My, my!" said Mrs. Pucker. "A cleaning lady. Aren't *we* getting fancy!"

"Well, well," said Mrs. Plum. "Did you check her references?"

"I didn't have to," said Mrs. Pinch. "She's coming from an agency. And she's highly recommended."

Meanwhile, at Old Howl Hall, Groad was getting ready to go to town.

"Wait for me!" called Moose Mummy, the Howls' cousin. He put on his smoking jacket and sunglasses.

"Grrr…," grumbled Groad.

Moose Mummy sat down in the front seat. "I'm ready!" he said.

"For what, you stupid moose?" growled Groad. "We're only picking up ze children from school and then going to get ze new cleaning lady at the bus stop."

Moose Mummy didn't say anything. He was staring at himself in the car mirror.

Groad rolled his eyes as he drove away

from Old Howl Hall. "Mummies!" he muttered. "They're so vain!"

Groad put on his blinker to make a left turn onto Main Street.

Just then, a big purple car came charging through the red light. It was heading right for Groad and Moose Mummy.

"Aaahhh!" screamed Moose Mummy.

Mrs. Pinch didn't even notice that she had nearly crashed into the Howls' car. She just kept driving at top speed toward Critter Falls Elementary.

Bruno Pinch was waiting for his mother in front of the school. He and his best friend J.D. were blowing spitballs.

"Watch this!" said Bruno to J.D.

Bruno put a piece of paper in his mouth and got it all wet and slimy. Then he put a plastic straw to his lips. He aimed and blew through the straw as hard as he could.

SPLAT. Bruno's slimy spitball hit Thistle right on the forehead.

"Ouch!" cried Thistle. She rubbed her forehead.

"Ha, ha, gotcha!" said Bruno.

Bruno and J.D. laughed at Thistle.

Just then, Axel and his friend Wilbur Jenkins came down the school steps.

"You'd better leave my sister alone," said Axel. He marched over to Bruno and J.D. "Or you're gonna be in big trouble."

"Yeah!" said Wilbur Jenkins. He pushed his glasses up on his nose. He glared hard at Bruno and J.D.

"We're so scared!" sneered Bruno.

"Yeah," said J.D. "Me and Bruno could clobber you two wimps with our hands tied behind our backs."

Just then Mrs. Pinch squealed to a stop in front of the school. "Let's go, Bruno!" called Mrs. Pinch. "We're late."

"See ya later," said Bruno to J.D.

"Bruno!" yelled Mrs. Pinch again.

Bruno hopped into the car. Mrs. Pinch peeled away from the curb and headed down Main Street.

The light changed from green to yellow.

Mrs. Pinch hit the gas and charged through the light as it turned red.

Groad and Moose Mummy were making the turn. Groad slammed on the brakes and skidded off to the side of the road just as Mrs. Pinch and Bruno went roaring by.

"Holy smokes!" exploded Groad. "Zere goes zat crazy Meesus Peench again! Where ees she going in such a beeg hurry?"

5

The Switcheroo

After Groad and Moose Mummy picked up Axel and Thistle, they headed over to the bus stop.

"Guess what's happening this Saturday afternoon?" Thistle asked.

Groad and Moose Mummy looked at each other and shrugged.

"I know!" said Axel.

"Shhh!" said Thistle, putting a finger to her lips. "Don't tell. Come on, guess!"

"I'm getting my hair

permed," said Moose Mummy. "My agent says a perm can make or break a movie star's career."

"No, that's not it," said Thistle. "Now you guess, Groad."

Groad smiled. "Zees Saturday I am making my famous grasshopper gumbo with jellyfish pudding," he said proudly.

"That's not the big thing that's happening either," said Thistle.

Groad frowned. "So what ees happening?" he asked.

"There's going to be a total eclipse of the sun," announced Thistle. "That's what."

"Eek lips?" repeated Groad. "What ees zat?"

"You know, when the moon blocks the sun and it gets dark and spooky outside," said Axel. "It's going to be really cool!"

Groad drove up to the bus stop just as the bus was pulling in.

"Does anybody know what our new

cleaning lady looks like?" Axel asked.

"I haf no idea," said Groad. He got out and opened the back door. "All I know is zat she ees coming from the agency and she ees highly recommended."

"Marvelous," said Moose Mummy. "I love meeting anyone who's recommended."

Groad glared at Moose Mummy. "Everyone follow me," he said.

Axel, Thistle, and Moose Mummy followed Groad through the crowd.

Suddenly, someone bumped into Groad.

"Pardon me," a bossy voice said.

"Ooof!" exclaimed Groad, stepping back. He couldn't believe his eyes. The voice belonged to none other than Mrs. Pinch!

Mrs. Pinch whacked Groad on the head with her purse. Then she marched onward to the bus. Bruno was right behind her.

"What are you doing here, jerk?" Bruno asked Axel.

"We're picking up our new cleaning

lady," said Axel. "And my name's not 'jerk.'"

"Whatever," said Bruno. "We're picking up *our* new cleaning lady, too. But I bet she's way better than *your* cleaning lady."

"Oh, yeah?" said Axel.

"Yeah," said Bruno, shoving his face right in Axel's face. The two boys stood nose to nose. Then Bruno stepped hard on Axel's foot.

"Ouch!" cried Axel.

At the same time, Thistle snuck up behind Bruno. She poured something down his pants.

"Help!" Bruno suddenly yelled, jumping up and down. "Something's biting me!"

"Bruno, stop clowning around and get over here!" called Mrs. Pinch.

Bruno ran to his mother. Wildly, he scratched at the seat of his pants.

"What happened to him?" Axel whispered.

"He's got ants in his pants," Thistle whispered back. She giggled. "I just happened to have some African Biter Ants that I brought in for show-and-tell." She held up the now-empty jar.

Axel grinned and high-fived his sister.

Just then, the bus doors opened. Zombie Mombie was the first one off the bus. She was carrying the shopping bag Dr. Del Ray had given her, along with a mop and pail.

It was the perfect cleaning lady disguise.

Mrs. Pinch saw Zombie Mombie's mop and pail. She began to wave her arms wildly in the air. "Yoo-hoo!" Mrs. Pinch called to Zombie Mombie. "Over here!"

Zombie Mombie headed over to Mrs. Pinch.

"Hello," said Mrs. Pinch. "I'm your new employer. And this is my son, Bruno." Mrs. Pinch pointed to Bruno. "Say 'howdy do,' Bruno, dear."

Bruno smiled a big fake smile. But as soon as his mother turned her back, he stuck out his tongue at Zombie Mombie. Zombie Mombie just stared at Bruno with glassy eyes.

"Now, what is your name?" Mrs. Pinch asked Zombie Mombie. The three of them made their way toward Mrs. Pinch's car.

"Zombie Mombie," said Zombie Mombie in a hoarse voice.

"Well, welcome to Critter Falls, Miss Mombie," Mrs. Pinch said.

By now, everyone had been picked up. Everyone except for a large woman in a long white coat, with a white hat on her head. She was surrounded by boxes.

Axel and Thistle looked at the woman in white. Then they turned to Groad.

"I bet that's our cleaning lady," said Thistle. "She looks weird."

Groad led the way down the platform toward the woman in white.

"Are you ze cleaning lady from ze agency?" asked Groad.

"Yes, I am," said the woman in white. "My name is Hilda Broom."

"Welcome, welcome," began Moose Mummy. He held out his hand toward Miss Hilda Broom. "Don't be shy. I may be a movie star, but—"

"These are my things," Miss Broom interrupted. She thrust one of her boxes at Moose Mummy.

"Boy, I wonder what's in all those boxes," Axel whispered to Thistle.

"It's my cleaning equipment," Miss Broom said, frowning. "Not that it's any of your business. Didn't anybody ever tell you that curiosity killed the cat?"

Axel and Thistle looked at each other. They raised their eyebrows.

"No, as a matter of fact," Thistle replied. "Anyway, cats have nine lives, so losing one life doesn't really hurt them."

"Harrumph!" exploded Miss Broom.

"Perhaps eet ees time to, umm…be going," interrupted Groad.

"Fine," said Miss Broom. She charged

toward the parking lot like a great white battleship. Carrying her many boxes filled with cleaning supplies, Groad, Moose Mummy, Axel, and Thistle all struggled to keep up with her.

They got to their car just as Mrs. Pinch, Bruno, and Zombie Mombie were driving away.

Zombie Mombie sat in the front seat next to Mrs. Pinch.

Mrs. Pinch peeked over at Zombie Mombie and smiled to herself. Her own cleaning lady! If only Louise Pucker and Beatrice Plum could see her now!

"Pee-yew!" Bruno suddenly piped up from the back seat. "Miss Mombie's got really bad B.O."

"Bruno!" exclaimed Mrs. Pinch. "How very rude! Now you apologize to Miss Mombie."

"Sor-ry," said Bruno. "But she really stinks."

Mrs. Pinch wrinkled her nose. She didn't want to admit it, but Bruno was right. Miss Mombie did smell rather...*ripe.* Still, manners were manners.

"That's enough, Bruno!" said Mrs. Pinch. She turned to Zombie Mombie. "I'm so sorry, Miss Mombie," apologized Mrs. Pinch. "You know how boys are."

Zombie Mombie didn't say a word. She only gripped the handle of her shopping bag all the more tightly. She glared at Bruno in the rearview mirror.

She knew just whom she was going to turn into a zombie first.

6

Out of Sight

That evening, Jack Howl retired to the drawing room. He walked over to the fireplace and stared at the portrait of Great-Grandpapa Howl that hung above the mantel.

"Why didn't you simply throw the Evil Eye away, old man?" Jack asked, puffing on his pipe. "Why did you hide it inside that silly flamingo statue?"

Suddenly, the eyes in the portrait came alive. And the lips moved. "Del Ray!" Great-Grandpapa Howl's portrait whispered.

Just then, Jack felt a hand on his arm.

He jumped.

"It's only me, dear," said Wanda.

"Did you hear that?" Jack asked Wanda.

"Hear what?" Wanda said.

"Great-Grandpapa just said something about 'Del Ray,'" said Jack. "Is it a person or a place, I wonder?"

"Dear," said Wanda, "I think you should stop worrying about the Evil Eye. It's perfectly safe for the moment."

"Well, let me just check on it one more time," said Jack.

"You've been checking on it every hour," Wanda reminded him.

"I know," said Jack. "But you can never be too careful with the Evil Eye."

Jack slid the portrait to one side. Underneath it was a black safe. Jack twisted the dial. The safe sprang open.

Inside were old photographs, a dusty trophy, plastic spoons, baseball cards, assorted other junk, and now...the Evil Eye. The amulet shone in the firelight.

Wanda peeked into the safe over Jack's shoulder. She smiled suddenly and reached inside for a big blue plastic cup. On the side it said: I ♥ CRITTERVANIA HIGH. "Remember this? We shared our first gopher guts soda in it."

"How could I forget?" Jack said.

"At least we know all of our valuable possessions are safe here," Wanda said.

Just then, the doors of the drawing room burst open. Axel and Thistle rushed in.

"We found Great-Grandpapa's trunk!" exclaimed Thistle.

"It's in the dungeon," said Axel. "And there's all this cool stuff inside."

The dungeon had once been Great-Grandpapa Howl's laboratory.

"Hmm," said Jack. "Maybe we'll find a clue somewhere in the trunk. Great-Grandpapa might have left a diary explaining about the Evil Eye."

The Howls hurried out of the drawing room. They passed Miss Hilda Broom in the hallway. She was wearing a doctor's white mask. She was sucking up all the cobwebs with a huge vacuum cleaner.

"Oh, dear!" Wanda suddenly exclaimed.

"What is it?" Jack asked.

"Miss Broom just sucked up my favorite

spider web," said Wanda. "You know, the nice big one by the stairs."

"How tragic!" Jack said. "It takes years to collect those cobwebs."

"And look what she's done with the dust," Wanda went on. "It's all gone! I've never seen a cleaning lady clean like this before."

"Odd," Jack said. "Very odd, indeed."

Down in the dungeon, they found Frankengator. Frankengator was the monster Great-Grandpapa had invented many years ago.

The monster was asleep on the table. He was lying on his back with his feet sticking up in the air. He was snoring loudly.

The Howls looked through the trunk. They found lots of strange and interesting things. They found a badminton birdie and a set of samurai swords. But there was no diary. And not a word about the Evil Eye.

"We tried," Jack said.

He closed the trunk with a loud bang.

The sound woke up Frankengator.

"Is it time for breakfast?" he asked.

"No," said Axel. "We were just looking for anything Great-Grandpapa might have written about the Evil Eye."

"Evil Eye," murmured Frankengator. He rubbed his eyes. "Great-Grandpapa left a letter. I remember he said to give it to you if you ever found the Evil Eye. Did you?"

"Yes, we did," everybody said at once.

Frankengator hopped off the table. He opened a cupboard. He pulled out a cookie jar. Inside was a dusty envelope.

Jack opened the envelope. Inside was a letter. He read it aloud:

"To my dear great-grandson Jack: If you are reading this letter, it means that you have found the Evil Eye. It also means that Dr. Del Ray, my sworn enemy, will soon be on his way to claim the Evil Eye for his own evil purposes. He will probably engage zombies to do his dirty work. So, if you should spot a zombie, rest assured that the evil doctor is not far behind."

"So that's why Great-Grandpapa's portrait uttered the name Del Ray," said Wanda.

"Yes, indeed!" said Jack. "There's a strange poem, too." He returned to the letter.

"When the moon and sun become one, and the day becomes as the night, then shall the Evil Eye lose its power of sight."

"What does that mean?" asked Wanda.

"That Great-Grandpapa was a lousy poet?" Jack suggested.

"I know!" Thistle exclaimed. "It's an eclipse! When the moon blocks the sun. We learned that at school."

"That's right," said Axel. "And this Saturday at exactly twelve o'clock, there is going to be a total solar eclipse."

"It only happens once every three hundred and sixty years," added Thistle.

"That explains why Great-Grandpapa never got rid of the Evil Eye," said Jack.

"He was waiting for the eclipse," said Wanda.

"We must be on the lookout for zombies, just as Great-Grandpapa warned us in his letter," said Jack. "Dr. Del Ray will surely be coming to claim the Evil Eye. And only we can stop him!"

7

Never Trust a Zombie

Back in Crittervania, Dr. Del Ray was rubbing his crystal ball. He wanted the crystal ball to show him what Zombie Mombie was up to in Critter Falls.

Suddenly, an image of Zombie Mombie appeared. She was in the Pinches' living room, sitting in Chief Pinch's recliner. Her feet were up on the coffee table. Her eyes were glued to the TV set. The Critter Cowboys were in the middle of a championship football game.

Empty pizza boxes and soda cans surrounded her. This wasn't Old Howl Hall!

"It cannot be!" Dr. Del Ray angrily struck his crystal ball. "That stupid zombie! She has gone to the wrong house!"

Just then the Pinches and J.D. appeared in the crystal ball. They were walking around the living room, staring straight ahead. Their eyes were glassy and their arms were extended before them.

"That idiot has turned the wrong critters into zombies!" yelled Dr. Del Ray, banging his hand on the table. "I should know better by now. You can never trust a zombie. I will have to go to Critter Falls myself to get the Evil Eye."

Dr. Del Ray's lips curled into an evil frown. Then he threw on his cape, grabbed his cane, and headed out the door.

Meanwhile, Zombie Mombie was having the time of her life. She was eating her way through the Pinches' kitchen. And now that she had turned the Pinches into zombies, they didn't bother her anymore!

Zombie Mombie stuffed a bologna and cheese sandwich in her mouth. Pieces of chewed bologna and cheese dribbled down her chin. Suddenly, the doorbell rang.

Zombie Mombie didn't get up to answer the door. She just sat staring glassily at the TV. The Critter Cowboys were in a huddle.

The doorbell rang again.

The Pinches and J.D. didn't seem to hear it. They just sat on the couch and looked straight ahead. Their eyes were blank. They stared at nothing. They were zombies, all right.

Just then, Mrs. Pucker and Mrs. Plum barged into the house. They looked at the mess. They looked at the cleaning lady drooling in front of the TV. They looked at their dear friend, Agnes Pinch.

"Agnes! Agnes!" exclaimed Mrs. Pucker, waving her hand in Mrs. Pinch's face. "What's wrong?"

Mrs. Pinch didn't say a word. She didn't move a muscle. She simply sat staring straight ahead.

"What in the world has happened?" Mrs. Plum asked in horror.

"And what is that awful smell?" asked Mrs. Pucker. She wrinkled her nose.

Zombie Mombie was beginning to get annoyed. Mrs. Plum and Mrs. Pucker were standing in front of the TV. They were blocking her view of the football game.

"Bruno! J.D.! Chief Pinch!" yelled Mrs.

Pucker. "What's wrong with all of you?"

Zombie Mombie had had enough. She reached into her shopping bag. First, she pulled out a glass bottle filled with a strange, sickly green liquid. Printed on the bottle were the words L'EAU DE ZOMBIE. Then she took out two frog skins and a watering can.

Suddenly, Zombie Mombie lunged toward Mrs. Pucker and Mrs. Plum.

Before the ladies could move, Zombie Mombie poured L'eau de Zombie over their heads. Then she

shoved a frog skin down each lady's back.

"Aaahhh!" screamed Mrs. Pucker and Mrs. Plum.

But Zombie Mombie was too strong and too fast for them. She sprinkled muddy water from the watering can over both of them. The water had been taken from a puddle at the Crittervania Cemetery at midnight, during the witching hour. And it was very powerful.

Instantly, a cloud of green bubbles rose up around the two ladies. When the bub-

bles cleared, Mrs. Pucker and Mrs. Plum stood before Zombie Mombie. Their eyes were glassy. Their arms were extended before them. Then they went to join the other zombies on the couch.

It was a full zombie house!

With a sigh of relief, Zombie Mombie climbed back into Chief Pinch's recliner. She reached for another sandwich. But there were none left! She had eaten every last crumb of food in the Pinches' house!

Zombie Mombie grabbed her shopping bag and headed out the door. Time to shop!

She marched down Main Street toward the Critter Falls Supermarket. Shopkeepers and customers tried to stop her from shopping. But she promptly turned each and every one of them into a zombie.

By the time she was finished with her shopping spree, there was barely a citizen left in Critter Falls who wasn't a zombie!

8

Scent of a Zombie

The next morning, Axel met Wilbur in front of their lockers at Critter Falls Elementary.

"Hey, don't forget about the eclipse tomorrow," Axel said.

"I know," Wilbur said. "I can't wait."

"It's gonna be really cool," Axel said.

Suddenly, Wilbur wrinkled his nose. "What's that smell?" he asked.

"Mmm," said Axel, sniffing. "Smells like a combination of rotten eggs and skunk. I love it!"

Just then, Bruno and J.D. came walking

down the hallway. Both boys were staring straight ahead. Their eyes were glassy and their arms were extended before them. And they were drooling!

"Pee-yew!" shouted the kids in the hallway. They all pinched their noses as the bullies passed.

"You guys really stink!" one of the kids shouted.

Everybody pointed at Bruno and J.D. and snickered. But Bruno and J.D. didn't say anything. They just kept walking.

"I don't believe it," said Wilbur to Axel.

"What's wrong with them?" asked Axel.

"I don't know," said Wilbur.

"Had a bath lately?" shouted another kid as Bruno and J.D. walked past him.

"No," said Bruno and J.D. without turning around.

"Gross!" someone else shouted. "You guys have bad breath!"

Axel and Wilbur looked at each other.

"Hmm...," said Wilbur, stroking his chin. "Glassy eyes, body odor, bad breath, drooling...You know what that sounds like to me?"

"What?" asked Axel.

"Zombification," said Wilbur. "Those are all the marks of a zombie."

Axel caught his breath. Great-Grand-papa Howl's warning! "I've got to tell my parents!" he shouted.

ew.

"What are you talking about?" asked Wilbur.

"There's no time to lose!" shouted Axel. "Dr. Del Ray must be on his way to get the Evil Eye!"

9

Dust
Buster

Axel took off down the hall. He ran out of the school building and rushed home.

When he got to Old Howl Hall, Miss Broom was in the hallway. She was dusting the grandfather clock with a blue feather duster.

"Where are my parents?" gasped Axel, fighting to catch his breath.

"I haven't the faintest idea," said Miss Broom, turning around. "All I know is that I have never seen a house in such a disgusting state in my entire life."

Suddenly, the grandfather clock opened its mouth and bit Miss Broom right on the bottom.

"*Ahhh!*" shrieked Miss Broom, jumping back in fright. "That clock just bit me on my bottom!"

"Now, Miss Broom," said Groad, walking into the hallway. "We have a lot to do in the kee-chen today. We must pluck ze legs off ze grasshoppers and skin ze jellyfish—"

"That does it!" shrieked Miss Broom. Before anyone could say another word, she ran out the front door of Old Howl Hall and disappeared down the driveway.

"Another one...how do you say in zees country?...bites ze dust," said Groad with a sigh. He wiped his hands on his apron. Then he went back to the kitchen.

Axel continued to search for his parents. He finally found them in the conservatory. Wanda was plucking the blooms off her roses. Moose Mummy and Frankengator were playing Chinese checkers on the floor. Jack was pacing back and forth, muttering about the Evil Eye.

"I win!" said Frankengator as he put his last piece into place on the board. He smiled happily. Frankengator loved playing checkers.

Axel burst out, "I saw two zombies! Bruno Pinch and J.D. are both zombies! Dr. Del Ray must be on his way!"

10

Walk Like a Zombie

As the sun rose over Critter Falls the next morning, Dr. Del Ray arrived. He strode down Main Street. Everywhere he looked, he saw zombies.

"That stupid zombie!" exclaimed Dr. Del Ray to himself. "She has turned every single critter in this town into a zombie, except for those confounded Howls. And we're running out of time!"

Dr. Del Ray marched up to the Pinches' house. He threw open the door. There was Zombie Mombie in the recliner, stuffing her face with pancakes and sausages.

"Stop eating at once!" commanded Dr. Del Ray. He knocked Zombie Mombie's platter of pancakes and sausages to the floor.

Still chewing, Zombie Mombie stared at Dr. Del Ray with glassy eyes. "Yes, Master," she said.

"We must get organized," said Dr. Del Ray. "The eclipse is going to happen in a matter of hours, and we must get the Evil Eye before then. I will lead the way. The rest of the zombies must follow. We will surround Old Howl Hall, turn the Howls into

zombies, and take the Evil Eye. Do you understand?"

"Yes, Master," said Zombie Mombie.

Over at Old Howl Hall, the Howls were on watch. They had spent the entire night barricading the house. And they were all in position. They were waiting for the arrival of Dr. Del Ray.

Axel and Frankengator were in the basement, by the dungeon door. Wanda and Jack were on the balcony. Groad was in the kitchen, watching the back door. Thistle was in the tower. And Moose Mummy was in the conservatory, overlooking the swamp.

Suddenly, Thistle spotted them coming down the road. It was an army of zombies. Dr. Del Ray was in the lead. Glassy-eyed and with their arms extended before them, the zombies marched toward Old Howl Hall. Thistle rang the tower bell.

"They're coming!" shouted Thistle. "Dr. Del Ray and the zombies are coming!"

She ran downstairs. "There are hundreds of them!" Thistle yelled.

Wanda clapped her hand over her heart. She turned to Jack. "What are we going to do?" she asked.

"We've got to distract them," said Jack.

"How?" asked Axel.

A slow, secret grin spread across Jack's face. "I have just the thing," he said.

11

Full Zombie House

Zombie feet clattered across the bridge. With glassy eyes and their arms extended before them, the zombies of Critter Falls marched toward Old Howl Hall.

But the sun was rising higher in the sky.

"Faster, zombies!" shouted Dr. Del Ray, the commander-in-chief of the zombie army.

"Yes, Master," the zombies droned as they quickened their pace.

Up the hill the zombies came, faster and faster. Down the long driveway leading to Old Howl Hall…faster still. Finally, they crashed through the barricades and then through the front doors of Old Howl Hall.

But the Howls were ready for them.

"Bring out the food!" shouted Jack.

Groad held high a platter of slugs in blankets. Moose Mummy held a pitcher of punch.

The zombies gobbled all the slugs in a matter of seconds, and Zombie Mombie drained the punch pitcher in one gulp.

The zombies marched past Groad and Moose Mummy. They wanted more!

Dr. Del Ray left the zombies to feed. He went in search of the Evil Eye.

The first door he tried was the bathroom. It was locked.

Aha! thought Dr. Del Ray. He smashed the lock with his cane and the door sprang open.

"Ahhh!" Frankengator screamed.

He jumped off the potty. His monster truck magazine flew up in the air.

Meanwhile, the sun was rising higher in the sky.

Jack and Wanda had slipped out of the house and into the cemetery.

Jack checked the sundial. In a matter of minutes, it would be time for the eclipse.

He pulled the Evil Eye out of his pocket. Carefully, he placed it on the sundial, exactly on the midday mark.

In the house, Frankengator, Moose Mummy, Axel, and Thistle all kept running back to the kitchen to bring out more and more platters of food. But the zombies were eating the food faster than they could set it down!

"Hey, look!" Thistle cried out, pointing. "The zombies! They're eating the furniture. That one just took a bite out of the couch." Thistle pointed to Mrs. Pinch, whose mouth moved up and down as she chewed the wood.

Mrs. Pucker was eating garbage right out of the garbage can.

And Mrs. Plum was munching on the curtains!

In the cemetery, Jack was pacing back and forth in front of the sundial.

"Where is Dr. Del Ray?" fretted Wanda.

"I don't know," said Jack. "But there's only one minute till the eclipse. We might just make it."

"Not so fast, Howl," said Dr. Del Ray, jumping out of the bushes. "Give me the Evil Eye—or die!"

12

Total Eclipse

Just then, the moon began to move across the sun. Everything was plunged into an eerie darkness. The wind started to blow and the temperature dropped. Strange-shaped shadows covered the ground.

The solar eclipse had begun!

"No!" screamed Dr. Del Ray.

He lunged for the Evil Eye and landed right on top of it, blocking it from the rays of the eclipse.

"No!" Wanda screamed.

"Ana…mana…manana!" Jack shouted as he grabbed Wanda. They both fell to the ground and covered their eyes.

At that moment, the Evil Eye sprang wide open. A strange, sickly green light engulfed Dr. Del Ray. Instantly, he was turned into a skeleton with bloody eye sockets.

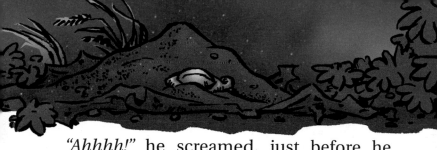

"*Ahhhh!*" he screamed, just before he was reduced to a pile of dust.

The moon now completely covered the sun. Darkness covered the still-opened Evil Eye. Slowly...slowly the Eye began to close.

Wanda and Jack watched as the Evil Eye shut for the last time...and was transformed into a beautiful, but harmless, piece of gold.

Axel and Thistle ran into the cemetery.

"The zombies!" shouted Thistle. "They're changing!"

Wanda and Jack followed their children into the house.

What they saw inside completely astonished them.

"Ze zombies all started turning back into creeters during ze eclipse," Groad explained.

Mrs. Pinch dropped the chair she had been eating. She spit out wood shavings. "Good heavens!" she shrieked. She turned to Mrs. Plum, who was still munching on the curtains. "Beatrice, why are you eating the curtains?"

"Look at Louise!" yelled Mrs. Plum, pointing to Mrs. Pucker. "She's licking the carpet!"

"How horrible!" yelled Mrs. Pinch. "Let's get out of here!"

All of the critters of Critter Falls fled from the house behind Mrs. Pinch.

"Hey!" said Thistle to Axel. "Look who's over there." She pointed to the corner of the room.

And there were Bruno and J.D., eating the tassels off the lamp as if they were pieces of spaghetti.

"Ptui!" They spit them out as they returned to their old selves.

"Let's get out of here," said Bruno to J.D.

"This place is creepy." The two boys walked quickly out of Old Howl Hall.

Suddenly, someone burped loudly. She was sitting in one of the armchairs.

"This one's still a zombie!" shouted Moose Mummy.

Everyone gathered around the chair.

"Well, of course," said Jack. "She's the original zombie. There's no way to turn her back."

Just then, Zombie Mombie opened her mouth and spoke.

"I stay and clean house," she said. "You need more dust. And cobwebs would look very good in this room. I do that for you."

"At last!" Wanda cried. "Good help. Someone who understands the concept of decorating with cobwebs."

"Very well," said Jack to Zombie Mombie. "You're hired."

Zombie Mombie smiled. "I do whole house, top to bottom," she said. "Except for one thing. Zombies don't do windows."